Inside were coloured pencils, paper, paint, paintbrushes, and a book filled with pictures of trees and animals Pikiq had never seen before.

"I'll draw them right away," he told Kri and Bou.
And that's just what he did—for hours and hours.

When Pikiq had used up all the
paper, he continued on the snow.

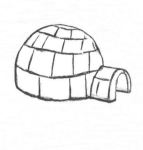

At the end of the day, Pikiq was very, very tired.

"Tomorrow," he said to Kri and Bou, "let's go on a trip and find those amazing animals and trees."

Then he fell fast asleep, dreaming about the
new trees and animals he'd seen in the book.

The next morning, Pikiq and his friends set out early.
They passed by Freko, a giant who had been dozing for
so long that grass and trees had grown all over him.

"May I bounce on your drum?" Pikiq asked
the giant's wife. Anitak smiled and nodded.

In the afternoon the three friends
came across a herd of caribou.

Mischievous birds led them into a maze
of antlers—and they almost got lost!

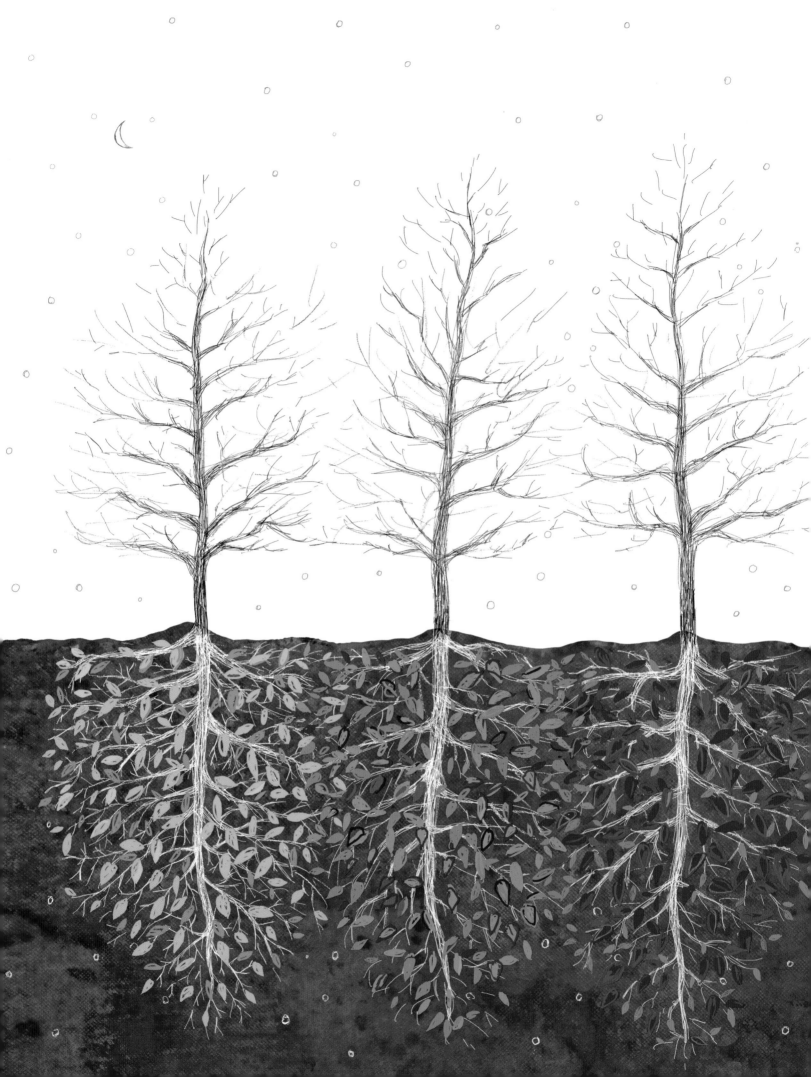

Then the friends played hide-and-seek with some trees.

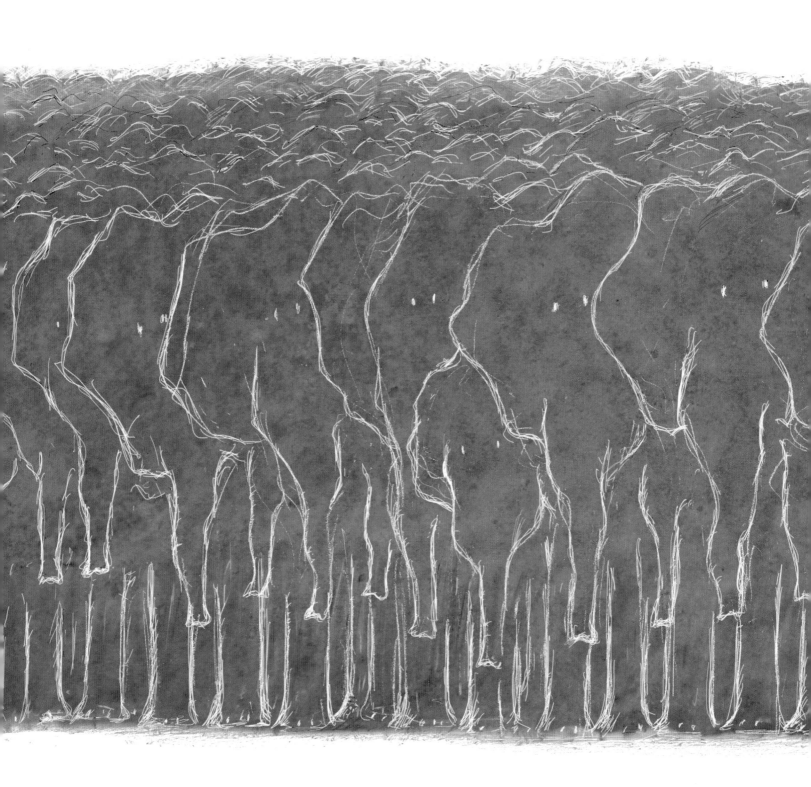

Later, Pikiq, Bou and Kri passed by a strange forest.

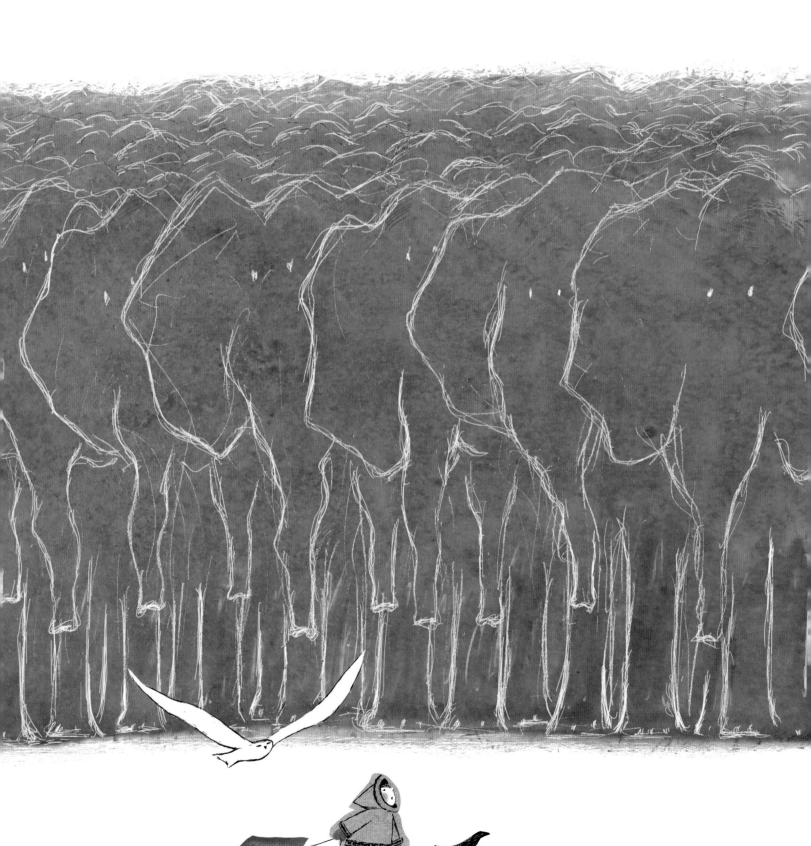

Soon the three friends spotted a banana plant.

Pikiq built a kayak with its huge leaves. "Let's go fishing!"

"Look, Bou!" Pikiq shouted. "I caught the moon!"

"Look, Kri! I'm flying!"

Pikiq soared with his friends to a turtle village.
On the horizon, a surprise awaited them.

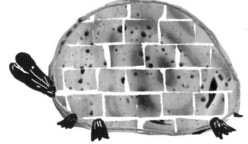

Around an inukshuk, Kri and Bou met
some friends from faraway countries.
While they played, Pikiq took a little nap.

When he woke up, everyone was
gone . . . except Bou and Kri.

"I had an amazing dream," said Pikiq. "I'll draw it right away!"

For Pablo's koinobori—Y

English translation published by Tradewind Books in Canada, the US and the UK in 2017
Text and illustrations copyright © 2015 Yayo
English translation copyright © 2017 Talleen Hacikyan
French edition published in 2015 by Les Éditions de la Bagnole

The publisher wishes to thank Julia Heller for her help with the English translation.

Book design by Elisa Gutiérrez

The text of this book is set in Mr Eaves Sans. Title type is Kabel.

10 9 8 7 6 5 4 3 2 1

. . . .

Library and Archives Canada Cataloguing in Publication

Yayo
[Pikiq. English]
      Pikiq / written and illustrated by Yayo ; translated from the French by Talleen Hacikyan.

Translation of French book with same title.
ISBN 978-1-926890-05-0 (hardback)

      I. Hacikyan, Talleen, translator II. Title. III. Title: Pikiq. English.

PS8597.A95P5413 2017   jC843'.54   C2016-905397-0

. . . .

Printed and bound
in Korea on ancient
forest-friendly paper.

MIX
Paper from
responsible sources
FSC® C023083

The publisher thanks the Government of Canada and Canadian Heritage for their financial support through the Canada Council for the Arts, the Canada Book Fund and Livres Canada Books. The publisher also thanks the Government of the Province of British Columbia for the financial support it has given through the Book Publishing Tax Credit program and the British Columbia Arts Council.

Canada Council
for the Arts

Conseil des Arts
du Canada

BRITISH
COLUMBIA
ARTS COUNCIL
Supported by the Province of British Columbia